Cl

Effect

Midwest Monsters Book 4

By Dakota Rebel

Supernova Indie Publishing Services, LLC

Copyright

© 2020, Dakota Rebel
Claus and Effect

Published by: Supernova Indie Publishing
Services, LLC

Warning: All rights reserved. The
unauthorized reproduction or distribution of
this copyrighted work is illegal. Criminal
copyright infringement, including
infringement without monetary gain, is
investigated by the FBI and is punishable by
up to 5 years in federal prison and a fine of
$250,000.

This is a work of fiction. Names, characters,
places and occurrences are a product of the
author's imagination. Any resemblance to
actual persons, living or dead, places or
occurrences, is purely coincidental.

Claus and Effect
by

Dakota Rebel

Anya –

There's something strange going on in Fayshore. I came to Michigan to visit my grandma for Thanksgiving. But the whole town is giving off super weird vibes. Everyone is pleasant enough, but I definitely feel like an outsider.

Good thing I found Nick. He's on vacation here, too. Though, the more time we spend together, the more I feel like he's hiding something as well.

Nick –

The holidays are my busiest season. I try to take a week off before the madness starts, and this year I decided to visit Fayshore. Ever since they came clean as a community about their supernatural status, every preternatural creature on the planet has wanted to visit.

Myself included.

It was just supposed to be a vacation. But then I met Anya and now I'm questioning my entire existence. I'd never had a problem being alone before. Now, the thought of leaving here without her fills me with dread. I don't know how she managed to turn my entire world on its head, but I know that I'll never survive without her.

Author's Note

Hello my darlings! I just wanted to pop in to wish you Happy Holidays! Or, if you're reading this in the summer, Happy July! Whatever…you do you.

This book was a hoot to write, but I want to give you fair warning that I definitely took some liberties with the folklore around Santa Claus.

It's not an instruction manual, or Norse Mythology. *Claus and Effect* is a fun little rom-com meant to entertain and make you smile. Let's not get hung up on the details.

I love you a bushel and a peck. Thank you for picking up Claus and Effect. If you love it, please consider leaving a review at your favorite book site.

Chapter One
~Anya~

I hadn't been to Fayshore, Michigan since I was a child. While growing up, my grandma had always come to visit us downstate. But she was getting older and I'd wanted to spend the holidays with her this year. So, here I was.

The town looked exactly as I remembered it. I'd always thought it was a fairy tale kind of place. With little shops dotting Main Street, friendly people walking around and waving at neighbors. It was like something out of a 1950's era television show.

Fayshore was already decorated for Christmas. Lights and boughs hung from the streetlamps, seeming a little out of place with the lack of snow or even chill in the air. It was unseasonably warm for November, but I appreciated that. Cold and I were not friends.

My phone told me to continue down Main to Airport and make a left at the light, but I spotted an adorable bakery and pulled into the lot, thinking I could pick up some sweets to take to Gran.

Entering the store, the smell of ginger and sugar felt like a warm hug, and a smile spread over my face from just the ambience. No wonder Gran had never wanted to leave. This place was too darling for words.

"Well, you must be Anya!" a plump woman behind the counter called out to me. She rushed around and stopped just short of hugging me. "You probably don't remember me at all. I haven't seen you since you were about ten years old."

"Dotty," I said, the name floating from the farthest recesses of my memory. "You used to sneak me snickerdoodles when my parents weren't looking! My goodness, you look exactly the same as you did fifteen years ago."

She beamed at me, then went ahead and thew her arms around me, hugging me tight to her ample bosom.

"You've grown up so pretty," she exclaimed, stepping back and cupping my jaw in her palm. "You look just like Evelyn when she was young."

"Thank you," I said, shuffling awkwardly on my feet.

"Evie told me you were coming for Thanksgiving. She's pleased as punch to see you again, let me tell you. It's all she's talked about for weeks." Dotty smiled again. "Sorry, where are my manners? What can I get for you love?"

She went back behind the counter and I browsed the glass case, torn at the amazing selection of sweets on display. As I oscillated between a pecan cake and a pumpkin roll, the bell over the door dinged behind me.

"Back again," Dotty said, her tone teasing toward whomever had walked in.

"I think you put something in those cookies, Dot," a deep male voice said.

Various parts of me stood at attention at the baritone, as if it had physically rubbed over my skin like velvet. I shuddered and couldn't help turning around to see the man that voice had come from.

"Good afternoon," the man said, nodding at me. "Stay away from the sugar cookies unless you're looking to be hooked. I swear I've gained eight pounds in the last four days."

He was tall, with broad shoulders and thick biceps. His red Henley was unbuttoned at the neck, the waffle stretched wide over his impressive body. His hair and tidy goatee were snow white, though he didn't look quite old

5

enough to have gone grey yet. Maybe mid to late forties. He had laugh lines around his twinkling blue eyes that crinkled deeper when he smiled at me.

Good grief, he was gorgeous…and I was staring at him like an idiot.

"Thanks for the advice," I said finally, a few beats after the silence had become awkward.

"Nick, don't tease my customers," Dotty admonished him. "Honey, you still need a minute?"

"Yes, please," I said, turning back to the case with heat burning my cheeks.

"How many?" Dotty asked Nick.

"Another dozen if you've got them," he answered.

"Just do," she said.

I watched as she cleared out the tray of perfectly round sugar cookies, with pink icing and sprinkles. They did look amazing and I was suddenly sad that Nick had taken the last of them.

Dotty handed him the pink bakery box and I turned to see Nick opening it to remove a cookie. He handed it to me and winked.

"First taste's free," he offered.

"I thought you said they were addictive?" I said, taking the offered sweet.

"I'm pretty sure that everything in here is," he admitted. "It's kind of a pick your poison situation."

"Well, thank you," I said, saluting him with the cookie.

I took a bite as I turned away from him, and the minute that sugary nirvana melted against my tongue, I let out a moan that seemed to come from my soul.

Nick inhaled sharply from beside me and I turned to meet his gaze. His eyes had gone from periwinkle to midnight and his tongue darted out across his lower lip. The move obviously unconscious but sexy enough to make my knees go weak.

"Really good," I said lamely, feeling the heat intensify in my face.

"Yeah," he agreed. "Uh, Dot, put it on my tab?"

"You got it," Dotty said, a smirk clear on her face.

"Ma'am." Nick nodded at me then turned and walked out of the shop.

"Well, that was fun!" Dotty said, clapping her hands. "How long are you in town for, Sugar?"

"Unclear," I said around a lump in my throat. What the hell was wrong with me? "My contract just ended with my job so I'm sort of between gigs at the moment. I guess I'll stay as long as Gran can put up with me."

"Oh, then you'll never get out of here." Dotty laughed heartily. "Now, what can I get for you? There's actually more cookies in the back, but Nick asked me to put him on rations two days ago."

"Well, I'll definitely take a dozen of those," I said immediately. "And let me get that pecan cake and the pumpkin roll. It's Thanksgiving, right?"

"Absolutely." Dotty puttered around, putting my sweets into boxes then bagging them up for me. I pulled out my credit card, but she shooed it away. "Evie would have my hide if I let you pay."

"Don't be silly," I insisted, thrusting the card toward her again.

"Oh, Honey." Dotty tsked and shook her head. "I can pretend to run it if it makes you feel better, but your money is no good here." She smiled at me again. "Baby girl, it's good to see you again."

"It's good to see you, too," I told her. And I meant it. "Uh, Dotty…"

"His name is Nick Kring," she said without waiting for me to actually ask. "He's here on vacation. Staying up at Mayor Colton's hotel. I think he's booked through the weekend."

"I'm sure I don't know what you're talking about," I said, but my smile probably gave me away. "Well, thank you for this. I'll see you soon."

"Bye, Sugar!" she called after me.

I drove the rest of the way to Gran's house with my thoughts consumed by the handsome silver fox I'd just met. Almost met. Damn it, I hadn't even given him my name.

It was absolutely ridiculous, but I really thought we'd had a connection there for a second. Even when I'd just heard his voice I'd been attracted to him. I'd never had much interest in anyone really. Celebrity crushes, I guess. But in high school I'd been a book nerd and didn't have time to date…not that anyone had been breaking down my door to take me out anyway. College was the same way.

I'd spent the last three years working on contract for an all-female tech school startup, so there weren't even any guys around me to be interested in. My friends were convinced I'd end up joining a convent any day now.

But Nick. Good lord. He melted something in me. Like a sugar cookie on my tongue. Thick and sweet and…

I pulled into Gran's driveway and forced my thoughts back to reality. We were just two strangers who had a moment, maybe, at a bakery. I'd probably never even see the man again. There was no point letting my brain run away with thoughts of sexy, white haired men. It was stupid.

Gran ran out onto the porch when she heard my car. When I got out she met me in the driveway and hugged me tightly, and I embraced her back. It had been a couple years since I'd seen her, but she looked great.

"How was your trip?" she asked, taking the bag of pastries from me while I grabbed my suitcase from the back seat. "No troubles?"

"Nope," I assured her. "Smooth sailing the whole way."

"Good." She beamed at me then headed toward the house. "I see you stopped by Dotty's."

"I did indeed," I agreed, following Gran inside. "She wouldn't let me pay."

"Good," Gran insisted. "You're my guest here. Speaking of which, how long can you stay?"

"As long as you can tolerate me," I promised her.

The phone rang and she apologized as she bustled off to answer it, and I made my way upstairs to put my suitcase away in my room.

When I opened the door, I couldn't help smiling at the familiar sight in front of me. Gran hadn't changed a thing in the room. The walls were still mint green wallpaper with tiny pink roses scattered across it. The quilt she made for me in grade school was spread across the bed, and the stuffed pony she'd won for me at a Halloween festival was nestled against a lace covered pillow.

It felt like I was walking into my home again for the first time in years. I blew out a happy sigh before tossing my suitcase into a chair, promising myself I'd unpack later.

When I got back downstairs Gran was off the phone and had cut the pumpkin roll into slices for us and had a fresh pot of coffee brewing on the counter.

"Come sit down," Gran insisted, carrying our plates to the table in her breakfast nook. "And tell me all about Nick."

Good grief.

Chapter Two
~Nick~

I hadn't been able to get the little blonde from the bakery out of my head. Her name was Anya, if I remembered correctly. She was the daughter of Sam and Danielle Detrich, which made her the granddaughter of Evelyn Detrich, who lived here in Fayshore.

We'd never met before, but I could recall that she'd been a very special child. Always well behaved, and always asked for books as gifts.

She'd grown up into a beautiful woman. Stunning really. The first woman to ever catch my attention as more than just a former name on a list. It had thrown me for a loop.

I got back to the hotel from the bakery and devoured the remaining eleven cookies as I thought about Anya. Where the hell were these feelings coming from? I wasn't a eunuch or anything, but I'd certainly resigned myself to spend the rest of eternity alone. I had a big job, a world of people depending on my focus. Dating just wasn't in the cards for me.

At least, it never had been. But maybe it was time to think about more than cookies and toys. Something inside of me had definitely seemed to awaken when I saw her. And when she'd moaned…well, something outside of me had woken up as well.

This was crazy. I was going home in a few days, and about to be so busy that I wouldn't have time to eat, let alone date. I was probably never going to see Anya again. It would be best to just put her out of my head now. No good could come from overthinking the situation.

My phone rang and I groaned when I saw it was my sister calling. She wasn't supposed to be bothering me while I was away. Which meant that there was a problem. I didn't want to deal with problems.

"Hey!" Hela said brightly when I answered. "How's the vacation going?"

"It was going great," I gruffed at her. "What's going on?"

"Nothing," she lied. "I can't just call to talk with my favorite brother?"

"You never do," I reminded her coldly. "What happened?"

"Fine." She blew out a sigh. "The gaming consoles are over a week late and the plant manager isn't returning my calls."

"Well, it's almost Thanksgiving," I said, relaxing a little. "They're probably shut down for the holiday. We can take care of it when I get back."

"You're awfully calm about this," she said, her tone suspicious. "Last year you went apoplectic when the train sets were seven hours behind their scheduled delivery."

"That was last year. And it was way closer to Christmas than this is." I shook my head. "Hela, why are you really calling?"

"The hourglass is glowing."

Silence fell between us for a full minute.

My mind began to race. The hourglass in the town square only lit up when there was a problem. Like a real issue. The last time it had happened was fifty-seven years ago when a snowstorm had blown in out of nowhere and almost grounded us on Christmas Eve.

And a hundred years before that, our village had contracted a virus and it has spread like wildfire, putting eighty percent of our workforce in bed for the entire first two weeks of December. Hela and I had never worked so hard in our lives to try to cover for the loss of hands in the shops.

"When did it start?" I asked, my voice hoarse.

"About an hour ago. It's faint, but it's definitely lit up." I could hear her chewing her lower lip as she always did when she was nervous. "Everything else is going like clockwork, so I thought maybe it was the game system delay."

"I don't think that's enough to cause an issue," I said. "Worst case I have to purchase them retail. There's nothing else going on there? No illnesses or injuries?"

"Nick, I'd have led with that if there was. How are you feeling? You're not getting sick are you?"

"No, I feel great." A knot began to form in my stomach. "You said an hour ago?"

"Yeah...why?"

I'd met Anya an hour ago.

No. No, there was no way this was related. It was just a very strange coincidence.

"Nick?"

"It's nothing," I insisted quickly. "Keep an eye on it and let me know if anything changes. I'll be home Saturday and we can look into it. That thing is almost two thousand years old, maybe it's just malfunctioning."

"Right," she said, the scorn so clear in her tone I could envision the massive eyeroll she'd just done. "Magic totems are funny that way."

"Hela, I've got to go. Call me if it gets brighter or you figure out what else is causing it, okay?"

"Yeah, alright."

She hung up and I dropped my cell on the table then opened my laptop. I went through the weather reports for all of the major cities in the world, but since Christmas was still so far out, none of them would be reliable yet anyway.

Damn it. I knew I should head home early. It wasn't an emergency yet,

24

but it probably wasn't something I could just ignore, either.

But I wasn't ready to leave. If I were being completely honest with myself, I wasn't ready to leave Anya. I wanted to see her again. It was ridiculous. I had no right, or even any reason, to be so enchanted with the young mortal. But she was stuck in my head, and I wanted to know her.

Being Santa had never been easy...but I had a feeling this year it was going to be hard as hell.

Chapter Three
~Anya~

"Gran, you seem pretty spry lately," I told her as I sat down to the massive breakfast she'd cooked for me the next morning. "What time did you get up?"

"I'm usually up around four," she admitted with a shrug. "I think it's the magic of Fayshore. I've felt better in the last four years than I've felt in decades."

"Small town living, huh?" I teased.

"Yeah, something like that." Gran patted my shoulder then walked around the table to sit across from me. "What are your plans today?"

"I don't know," I admitted. "I thought we could visit and catch up."

"That sounds lovely," Gran said, beaming at me. "But I have a Bridge game at eleven. Maybe you could explore the town on your own for a little while?"

"Yeah. I can do that." I took a sip of my coffee and smiled over the rim. "Seriously, you look great."

"You're a peach." She waved away my compliment. "While you're out, would you mind stopping at the store and picking up a few things for me?"

"Not at all," I agreed. "Stuff for Thanksgiving?"

"Oh, no." She shook her head. "I hope you don't mind, but we'll be going to dinner at the mayor's house. They have

28

a huge dinner for anyone who wants to come and it's always such a wonderful time."

Wow, this town was really tight knit. I'd never even met the mayor of our town. But here they all got together for holidays? That was so sweet.

"No, I don't mind at all. It will probably be better than cooking a big meal just for the two of us."

"And no clearing up." She winked. "Well, you should eat. I'm going to get ready."

I dug into a stack of pancakes as she went upstairs. Man, she really did look ten years younger than the last time I'd seen her. It was crazy. I mean, she'd never been exceptionally old to me. Gran was the most energetic woman I'd ever known. But now…I don't know. It almost did seem like magic how vibrant she seemed.

When I couldn't eat another bite, I took the dishes to the kitchen and cleaned up. By time the last dish was dry Gran was back downstairs, wearing a pink tracksuit with rhinestones at the collar.

"Well, look at you!" I said, grinning at her. "This must be a fancy Bridge game."

"Not exactly black tie," she teased. "But we like to get dolled up on occasion. Now!" She clapped her hands and pulled a list out of her purse. "Just have this and anything you'd like to have around the house put on my tab. There isn't a store in town that hasn't been warned not to take your money."

"Gran," I complained.

"I've got more money than I can spend before I pop my clogs," she insisted. "And anything that's left is going to you anyway, young lady. Don't argue with me, I've got more experience."

"Yes ma'am." I blew out a sigh. "Well, have fun. Is there anything you'd like to have for dinner tonight?"

"We'll just order a pizza." She shrugged then leaned forward and kissed my cheek. "Have a nice day, darling."

"Bye." I watched her walk outside and blew out a laugh. Spry old bird.

I grabbed a cookie off the plate on the counter and as soon as I took a bite my thoughts instantly snapped back to meeting Nick at the bakery. He was so handsome. Like…unreasonably so.

For a moment I seriously considered devouring the rest of the sweets to have an excuse to go back to Dotty's and maybe run into him again.

What the hell was wrong with me? He was just a nice man that I'd shared a brief moment in time with. And we were both only here for vacation. What good was going to come from giving in to a crush on a man I was never going to see again?

Nothing, I decided. Best to forget all about him. I wasn't a head in the clouds kind of girl, and I wasn't about to start now. People don't just fall for each other in a second. I was fascinated by him, sure. But that was all it was.

****

I walked into the grocery store later that morning and smiled at the opening bars of *Santa Claus is Coming to Town* blaring over the loudspeaker. It had always been my favorite holiday song. A million times better than *Christmas Shoes*. Ugh. Christmas songs should be happy, damnit.

After grabbing a shopping cart, I wandered up and down the aisles, tossing things from Gran's list into the basket along with anything else that looked good. Mostly candy, to be honest. I'd always had a wicked sweet tooth, and it seemed I would be giving in to baser instincts over the holidays.

When I'd finished, I got in line behind two young women with a heaping cart of groceries.

"You should go ahead of us," the dark-haired woman said, when she noticed my modest amount of goods.

"Don't be silly," I said, waving her offer away. "I'm in no rush. Plus, I'm digging the music."

"You must be Anya," the red-haired girl joined in, looking me up and down. "Evie's granddaughter."

"Goodness, did she tell everyone I was coming?" I asked with a laugh.

"Pretty much," the first woman agreed. "I'm Mindi, this is my sister Candi."

We all shook hands then they began to put their groceries on the belt.

"Anya," I said then laughed. "Obviously. You must be having a pretty big Thanksgiving dinner."

"For sure," Candi agreed. "We throw a party for most of the town every year."

"Oh! At the mayor's, right? Gran said we'd be going this year."

"That's wonderful!" Mindi said, clapping her hands. "Our sister is married to Colton…uh, Mayor Steele. We offered to come pick up the rest of the food today."

"Yeah, any excuse to get away from the kids," Candi agreed with a soft laugh. "We both have twin toddlers. I'd offer to mow town square if it got me twenty minutes of quiet."

"Wow!" I felt my eyes widen in surprise. "You both have twins."

"Well, we're triplets, so multiples run in the family," Mindi explained. "But yeah, with our two and Mindi's three...it gets a little wild."

My mind reeled at that. Seven kids between them. That sounded...like a lot of kids.

Candi cackled and reached over to squeeze my arm, nodding. "Yeah, it's a mess. But damn, it's fun."

"Hey!" Mindi said excitedly. "You should come out with us tonight. Our aunts are taking the brats for the night to give us a break. We're just going to grab a couple drinks, but it should be a good time."

"That's very sweet," I said, surprised by the offer. "Everyone here is so friendly."

"We're a pretty close-knit community," Candi agreed. "Come out with us."

"Maybe," I said, biting my lower lip. "I just got here. I don't want to abandon Gran already."

"Bring her along," Mindi said with a shrug. "She's a hoot."

"I'll ask her," I promised.

They paid for their groceries and left after telling me the name of the bar they'd be at. This place was crazy. Granted, being from a big city I didn't know much about small town life. But I'd never seen so many people be so friendly to literally everyone. I didn't know if I could ever get used to it.

When I got back to the house, Gran had returned and was in the living room, curled into a chair with a book.

"Did you have a nice day?" she asked, getting up to help me put the groceries away.

"I did," I admitted with a smile. "I met a couple girls that invited us out to the bar tonight."

"Oh, you should go!" Gran insisted. "Meet some people your own age."

"Is this a conspiracy?" I asked, narrowing my gaze at her. "Did you tell the town to be extra nice to me?"

"Why would I do that?" she asked.

"I don't know," I admitted with a shrug. "I already told you I'll stay as long as you want me to. You don't need to bribe me with friends and cake."

"I can assure you that I've done no such thing." Gran shook her head. "You're so much like your mother. Unable to accept a gift without wrenching the horse's mouth open. Go make some friends. Have a few drinks. Maybe you'll run into your handsome man again."

"Enough of that," I snapped. "I told you last night, Dotty had no right to insinuate that anything had happened. He gave me a cookie."

"Yes, dear," she said, her eyes sparkling. "It wouldn't hurt you to find a boyfriend, you know. I understand that you worked yourself to death in school. But baby girl, you're not getting any younger."

"Thank you for that," I said. "And maybe I am. It seems that you are."

She laughed again then patted my arm. "Go out tonight. Please."

"Okay," I agreed. "I think I will."

But it wasn't because I secretly hoped she was right, and Nick might be there. It was because it would be nice to spend time with some women my own age.

Oh, I was such a liar. Of course, I hoped I'd run into Nick again. Gran was right, I certainly wasn't getting any younger. And maybe it had been fate that the moment I got to town I ran into the first man who had ever held my interest.

Or maybe I was just a crazy person.

Chapter Four
~Nick~

"How are you enjoying your stay, Nick?" Colton asked as he slid onto the stool next to me at the bar.

"It's wonderful," I admitted. "You've got a hell of a town here, Mayor."

"Thank you," he said, smiling as his gaze scanned the bar. "It is pretty special."

"Were you scared?" I asked, unable to hold back the question.

"What?" He turned back to me. "Oh, you mean the reveal." He shrugged.

"Yes and no. The magic of the town would have protected the supernaturals if the time wasn't right. I was more worried it wouldn't hold. But it's been amazing. The ability for everyone to be who they really are. It's like everyone finally exhaled at once."

"I would imagine." I smiled at him. "You made quite the impression on the supernatural community."

"Apparently," he said, grinning. "If news reached you all the way at The Pole it must have made some pretty wide ripples."

"The first town to show itself to the normals?" I laughed. "Yeah, you could say it rippled pretty far."

The energy of the room shifted so hard my body actually rocked. Colton didn't seem to notice at all, his posture relaxed as he ordered a beer for himself and another drink for me as well.

What the hell had just happened? I looked around and when my gaze turned to the door, I swore under my breath.

Anya had just walked in.

She was with the mayor's wife and her sisters, and she didn't seem to notice me. I watched as they walked toward an empty table at the back. When they sat down, I lost sight of her through the crowd, though.

"You okay?" Colton asked, his gaze narrowing. "You look a little…less than jolly."

"Can I ask you an incredibly personal question that is absolutely none of my business?" I didn't want to ask him, but my physical reaction to Anya, coupled with my worries about the hourglass, meant that I couldn't really dick around with this. Something was happening, and I didn't understand it.

"Sure," he agreed, turning to face me. "Do you want to go somewhere private?"

"No, it's not…not like that." I blew out a sigh. "How did you know Trudi was the one? From what I understand, you only got one shot at a life mate. And you're both really young." Of course, to me, most creatures were incredibly young. "How did you know it was right?"

"Well," he said, smiling softly. "Our magics just clicked. The first time I saw her, I just knew she was it for me. We both fought against it, but when you meet your soulmate…there's no amount of pushing you can do to change fate's mind."

That made sense. Of course, their magics would recognize each other as compatible life mates. Unfortunately, Anya didn't have magic. She was a normal. A nice, young mortal girl who would grow old and pass on as mortals do.

There was absolutely no way that she was my fated mate. In fact, I kind of doubted I would have one. If I'd been on this realm for this long, and never found the one, it was unlikely that a chance encounter at a bakery was going to alter my fate now.

"Have you met someone?" Colton asked softly. "Since we're getting personal."

"I don't think so," I said quickly. "I just don't think it's in the cards for me."

"Old man, it's in the cards for everyone." He patted my hand. "Maybe you just had to wait a little longer than the rest of us. But you'll get there."

It was a pretty thought, kind words from a kind man. But not me. Another hundred years from now I would look back fondly on the young woman who had pulled at my heartstrings for a moment in time. That's all this was.

Best to forget and move on. I should probably go home early, actually. With Hela's worrisome call, and the distractions here, I needed to get back to The Pole and check on things.

"You're coming to Thanksgiving tomorrow, right?" Colton asked, pulling me out of my thoughts.

"I don't know," I said. "That really seems like a town affair. I don't want to gate crash."

"Don't be ridiculous," Colton insisted. "Everyone wants to meet you. You're quite a celebrity and, selfishly, my children would love me more if they got to see you."

"Well, hard to turn down an offer like that," I agreed with a laugh. "If you're sure, then that would be lovely. But I think I'll be going back home early. I've very much enjoyed my stay in Fayshore, and I'll certainly be back. But there are things that I need to attend to."

"That's a shame," he said, and he looked as if he really meant it. "You've been a wonderful guest, and of course we'd be thrilled to have you back any time."

"Hello boys," Trudi said as she approached us. "Look at you two, sitting here all anti-social."

"Look at you," Colton said, beaming at his wife as he slid to his feet and kissed her cheek. "I hardly recognize you without urchins hanging from your limbs."

"I know!" she agreed before turning to me. "Nick. Lovely to see you again."

I stood as well and took her offered hand, bowing over it respectfully.

"Colton, darling, I want you to meet our new best friend. She's absolutely darling and I want you to convince her to move here."

"That's not really what I do," Colton said, narrowing his gaze at his wife. "Does she know?"

"Not yet," Trudi said. "But she'll fit right in. Come now. Nick, you as well, please."

Trudi walked away, not looking back as if she just expected us to follow her. Which we did. I knew exactly who this friend was, and while I wanted to run out the front door rather than face her again, I fell in step behind Colton.

"Anya, sweetie, this is my husband, Colton. Colton, meet Anya Detrich. Evie's granddaughter."

"Pleasure," Colton said, shaking hands with the beautiful blonde. "How are you enjoying Fayshore?"

"It's a bit overwhelming," Anya admitted with a soft laugh. "Everyone is so nice. Oddly so. Hard for a city kid to adjust to."

"You'll get the hang of it," one of Trudi's sisters insisted from her seat next to Anya. "If you stay."

"Ladies, have you had the opportunity to meet Nick Kring?" Colton said, grabbing my arm and pulling me forward.

Chapter Five
~Anya~

I sucked in a breath so loud that everyone at the table turned to stare at me. I tried to turn the sound into a light cough but saw the look Mindi and Trudi traded between themselves.

Nick shook hands with Candi and Mindi then turned his bright, blue gaze on me.

"Lovely to see you again," Nick said, smiling warmly at me as I got to my feet and held my hand out.

When our palms touched, a sharp shock sparked between our skin and made me jump back in surprise.

"Wow, staticky in here," I laughed, rubbing my hand up my arm.

The conversation between the mayor and the LaFey triplets halted abruptly as they all turned their gazes on me and Nick again. It was a little creepy how they all turned their heads in unison, actually.

"Yeah," Nick agreed, his eyes darkening visibly even in the dimness of the bar.

"How is your vacation going?" I asked him lamely. God, why was I so awkward around him?

"Well," he said, clearing his throat. "Almost over, actually. But it's been nice here."

"Yeah," I agreed. I looked around the table again, but the women had averted their gazes from us and resumed their family conversation. "It's a lovely town."

"It certainly is lovely," Nick agreed. "Well, ladies, Colton." He bowed his head. "I should get going."

"I'll walk you out," Colton said, clapping Nick on the shoulder. "Anya, lovely to meet you. Ladies."

They walked away and I felt my cheeks burning with embarrassment when I turned back to the table to see all three women staring at me with matching smiles on their faces.

"What was that?" Candi asked, leaning forward.

"What was what?" I asked.

"Uh, Nick," Mindi said pointedly. "You've met already?"

"Yeah." I shrugged. "We ran into each other at Dotty's bakery when I first got to town. He gave me a cookie."

The triplets exchanged a look.

"It was nothing," I insisted.

"That was not nothing," Candi said. "You guys literally sparked off each other."

"It's dry in here," I said, rolling my eyes. "I could shuffle my feet and shake your hand, see if we hit it off."

The girls all laughed, and Candi held her hands up defensively.

"He's quite handsome," Mindi said after a minute. Her sisters looked at her with identical raised eyebrows. "What? I'm married, not dead."

"He is handsome," I agreed. "But lots of men are."

"You like him," Trudi said softly.

"I don't even know him," I argued feebly. "We're both in town for a limited amount of time and it's just one of those things."

"Nothing that happens in Fayshore is *one of those things*," Candi argued.

"What does that mean?" I asked with a confused laugh.

"Nothing," Trudi insisted, cutting off whatever Candi was about to respond with. "She's drunk."

"I am not!" Candi said, shoving her sister. "I'm just saying...don't give up just yet. Okay?"

"There's nothing to give up on," I said firmly. "Can we please stop talking about Nick?"

"Of course," Mindi agreed calmly.

Silence fell heavy over the table for a few minutes. I glared at the women and we all broke into giggles.

"Seriously," I said with a sigh. "We are four attractive, intelligent women. We can't find anything else to talk about?"

"It's just…that spark," Candi said, her tone a little wistful. "That's pure magic right there, sweetie. Best not to ignore it."

"Magic?" I raised an eyebrow. "Surely you don't believe in such nonsense?"

The three women exchanged a look between themselves.

"Everyone needs a little magic in their lives sometimes," Trudi said softly. She lifted her shoulders in a small shrug.

That was probably true. It wasn't as if I could deny that I liked him at this point. He fascinated me. And yes, the physical spark between us had been a little strange. But none of that changed the fact that he was leaving in a few days.

I didn't know what to do, but I knew for sure I wasn't about to start a fling with an expiration date. My first time was not going to be with a man I had no chance of pursuing a real relationship with. That just wasn't how my heart, or my mind worked.

So, I would admire him from a distance. Safer for everyone involved.

"Let's do shots!" Candi insisted loudly, raising her hand to get the waitresses attention. "Everyone just got way too serious."

"I really shouldn't," I said quickly. "I have to drive back to Gran's."

"We'll get you a ride," Trudi assured me. "You're on vacation, right? Well, so are we. A night without the brat pack is a rarity. So, let's drink and become lifelong friends."

Hard to argue with that, I supposed. I very much liked these women, and I didn't have many friends back home. It would be nice to just let go and have some fun.

Though I have to admit, when Candi ordered the fourth round of tequila shots, I started to question what kinds of friends I was making here. The room had taken on a very warm glow and at one point, I was sure I'd seen a lemon wedge fly across the table on its own and smack Mindi in the face.

"Okay," I said, shaking my head. "I'm thoroughly toasted."

"One more," Candi begged.

"No, ma'am," I said, getting to my feet and finding them a little wobbly. "I'm going to need that ride home now."

"Your chariot awaits," Nick said from beside me. "Shall we?"

Chapter Six
~Nick~

I watched Anya glare around at the sisters, who were not even trying to contain their laughter. But when the blonde turned back to me she was smiling.

Obviously the LaFeys hadn't told her I would be the one to drive her back to her grandmothers. She had the same reaction I'd had after Colton insisted we go back to his place for drinks, then commenced to getting himself good and drunk. I hadn't realized at the time that he was ensuring he would be unable to drive anywhere.

Alcohol doesn't affect me the way it does others, so of course I was perfectly sober and apparently the only available chauffer for Anya.

This family was entirely too meddlesome for their own good.

I helped Anya to my rental car and into the passenger seat. When I slid behind the wheel she rolled her head over to look at me.

"They're all menaces," she said. "Sorry you got roped into this."

"It's not a hardship," I assured her. "I quite enjoy your company."

"I like you, too," she whispered. "But I decided tonight that I can't kiss you."

"I wasn't aware that was on the table," I teased as I pulled out onto Main Street, following the directions Colton had given me.

"Because," she continued as if I hadn't said anything. "I think I could fall for you Nick Kring."

My grip on the wheel tightened as she spoke. She was intoxicated, and probably completely unaware of what she was saying. I certainly wasn't going to encourage her, but I couldn't make myself ask her to stop talking.

"It's not just that you're handsome," she said, turning her head to look away from me. "There's something about you. A kindness. A presence. Like I know you somehow. You feel…like home to me. I don't understand it. But I like it very much."

"Anya," I said, my voice hoarse. "Perhaps you shouldn't—"

"If you weren't leaving this place," she said. "It might be different. The worst part of all of this is that I think you feel it, too. If it was one sided, it wouldn't bother me so much. I mean, we don't even know each other. It's ridiculous to think I have feelings for you."

"Is it?" I asked, unable to bite back the question.

"I've never even kissed a man before," she admitted. "How could I possibly know…"

She trailed off and I forced myself not to ask her to go on. She was right. I was leaving. Nothing could come of this. She was young. She was mortal. We were both woefully inexperienced. I had no right to feel anything for her. Nor her for me.

I pulled into the driveway and put the car in park, staring forward at the house. My heart was pounding in my chest and the need to pull her into my arms and hold her tight was overwhelming.

"I'm sorry," she whispered.

"Whatever for?" I asked, finally turning to look at her, my eyes wide with surprise at her apology.

"Because I'm very drunk." She smiled softly, tears glittering in her eyes.

"So, you probably don't believe a word that I'm saying."

"That's not it," I assured her. "I do believe you. And you're right, I do feel it as well. But you *are* drunk." I reached over and ran a finger lightly over her chin. "And I *am* leaving."

Her fingers entwined with mine and she pulled our hands to her lap, staring down at them as a tear rolled down her face.

"I should get inside," she said, sniffing lightly. "Thank you for driving me home."

I pulled her hand to my lips and pressed a soft kiss to the back of it. Her gaze met mine for a moment and as we stared at each other, I knew I was lost.

She smiled, then pulled her hand free and got out of the car. I watched her walk up the stairs and into the house without turning back again. When the door closed behind her, I blew out a heavy sigh and backed the car out of the driveway, headed back to the hotel.

Colton was going to be getting a very angry wake-up call from me in a few hours.

****

"I think you're being ridiculous," Colton insisted as I helped him carry chairs to the dining room the next afternoon. "She's a lovely girl. You two could be very happy together."

"She is a very young, mortal girl," I reminded him coldly. "With a whole human life ahead of her. With friends and family that I have no right to take her away from."

"I think fate has taken this decision out of your hands," he said kindly.

We were setting up for the big Thanksgiving dinner at their home, and the women were all in the kitchen cooking while their husbands and I did the grunt work.

"I remember when Candi first came to town," Lincoln said wistfully. "We fought like cats and dogs and I was half-dead with need for her. I thought there was no way I'd ever find another woman that made me feel the way she did." He shrugged. "Turned out I didn't have to.

Being married to her is the best thing that ever happened to me."

"Yes, but she's a witch," I reminded Lincoln. "You've all met your supernatural matches. I can't love her then lose her in another fifty or so years. What kind of gift is that from fate?"

"I could turn her into a vampire," Booker, Mindi's husband, offered.

"That's very kind," I said, laughing. "But no. This is ridiculous. We shouldn't even be talking about this. The decision has been made. By both of us. So, let's just move on."

By the time guests started to arrive for dinner, the entire downstairs of the home had been transformed into a Christmas wonderland. I'd added a few of my own touches to make it almost, but not obviously magical.

I'd thought the group would have wanted more of an autumn theme for Thanksgiving, but the LaFey women had been adamant that they wanted it to look as if my own personal home had thrown up in their living space, so I had agreed happily.

The moment Anya and her grandmother walked into the room I felt her, without having to even look up. Her presence absolutely screamed to me and I was powerless to avoid her.

I turned to see her speaking excitedly to Mindi, one of the triplet's toddlers already perched on Anya's slender hip. She looked really good with a baby in her arms and my cock twitched in interest at the thought of…

"No," I muttered.

"What was that, old man?" Colton asked, knocking his shoulder against mine as he stood next to me.

"Meddlesome," I gruffed at him, stalking over to the door to greet Anya and her grandmother.

"Mrs. Detrich," I said, bowing to the older woman first. "Nick Kring."

"Naturally," she said, looking me up and down and smiling. "Lovely to meet you. You must call me Evie, everyone does."

"Evie," I agreed with a smile. "Anya," I said, turning my gaze to her.

"Nick." She nodded to me, her cheeks blazing pink.

"Well," Evie said, clapping her hands before taking the child from her granddaughter's grip. "I must say hello to our hosts. If you'll excuse me."

She bustled away, leaving Anya and I alone for the moment.

"I'm very sorry about last night," Anya said quickly, obviously blurting it out before she lost her nerve. "I shouldn't have said those things to you."

"Did you mean them?" I asked.

"I did," she agreed, dropping her gaze to the floor. "But I had no right to share my feelings with you."

"Anya," I whispered. I put a finger under her chin and lifted her face back to look at me. "I'm very glad you did. Things between us are…strange. But while I'm here, I hope that at the very least we can have honesty between us."

Which was easy to say, but the thought of expressing my true feelings to her terrified me. I was going to fall in love with this woman. And I was going to leave her here. How the hell do you explain that to anyone?

"Okay," she agreed. "Will you sit with me? At dinner?"

"I'd be delighted." I offered her my arm and she took it, allowing me to lead her into the dining room where the guests were congregating.

This was a huge mistake. I knew it, but I couldn't stop it. I only had a couple days left, and I intended to spend as much time with her as possible. Even if it shattered my heart and my soul when I had to leave her.

Chapter Seven
~Anya~

I'd been horribly nervous to face him at dinner on Thanksgiving, but I should have known he'd be a perfect gentleman about the entire drunken conversation the night before. In fact, he'd pretty much admitted he felt the same way I did. Torn, scared, and regretful that our time together would be so short.

We'd sat together for dinner and had a lovely conversation about nothing at all really. After we'd eaten, both of us tried to help clean up, but Colton and the triplets assured us that it would be taken care of and shooed everyone into the ballroom for refreshments and dancing if anyone chose to.

The party was lovely, the guests were sweet to everyone, even me. I still felt like an outsider though. They all knew each other, and they all even seemed to know Nick well, stopping by our table to shake hands with the older man.

Gran had left with her friends shortly after dinner was cleared away, after ensuring that Nick wouldn't mind driving me back to her house. I'd been a little hesitant to accept his forced offer, after making such a fool of myself the night before, but I honestly wasn't ready to leave yet, so we'd all agreed to the arrangement in the end.

Around eight p.m., Colton and Trudi came over to us, each with matching sheepish grins on their faces.

"I'm so sorry to bother you," Trudi said to Nick. "You are our guest, but the children are requesting that you tell them a bedtime story. Would you mind?"

"Of course not!" he said, a genuine grin lighting his face. "Shall you bring them here?"

"Oh, that would be wonderful," Trudi said, clapping her hands. She turned to her husband. "Make sure everyone has a drink darling, I'm going to wrangle the beasts."

I watched in fascination as Nick strode to the middle of the room, placing a chair in the center of the dance floor while the whole town gathered around him. The army of children, most of them belonging to the LaFey triplets, ran to Nick, dropping to the floor in front of him, their little faces bright and excited to hear whatever story the older man was about to share.

"What would you like to hear tonight?" Nick asked the kids, his blue eyes twinkling as he took them all in.

"Tell us about the North Pole!" a brave little girl begged as she grinned up at him.

"The North Pole you say?" Nick chuckled and nodded. "Very well. Shall I tell you the story of the actual pole?"

He settled back in his chair, and from the very first word out of his mouth, everyone in the room, adults and children alike, listened with rapt attention.

"Seventeen hundred years ago, life was very different for all creatures on earth. There was no electricity, no video games or television. No cars. There were just families. One such family were the Claus family." He paused to take a drink, the moment of silence drawing people closer in anticipation.

"Santa and his sister built a factory at the highest point of the world. They wanted nothing more than to bring the utmost joy to the people of the realm during the darkest and dreariest point of the year. So, they gathered any and all toymakers that would come, to make gifts for children."

The kids watched Nick with absolute reverence on their faces as he spun his tale, and the adults were just as enchanted. He had a voice that seemed made for speaking, and his story was so adorable, none of us could help but hang on his every word.

"The pole itself, is actually a lever," he continued. "Did you know?"

The children all shook their head, and I found myself also moving my head, right along with them.

"This lever turns the hourglass. In the very center of town, we have our own sort of advent calendar. A massive hourglass filled with 366 diamonds. The lever turns the hourglass every year on December 26th, counting down the days until the next Christmas."

"How does it know about leap year!" one of the older kids asked.

"Magic." Nick touched the side of his nose and winked at the child. "The truly amazing thing about this hourglass, is its ability to warn Santa if there are dangers. If something threatens to upset Christmas plans, it will begin to glow." His gaze lifted and his eyes met mine across the room. "It's glowing right now. Very faint, but it's there."

"What's wrong?" a little girl asked, her tone thick with emotion.

"Maybe people don't have enough Christmas spirit this year," Nick said. He opened his arms and she climbed up into his lap, burying her face into his shirt. "So, before you go to sleep tonight, maybe you could all write your letters to

Santa. Remind him who he's working for. Remind him that nothing can really stop Christmas. Because Christmas lives in here." He touched the little girl's chest, over her heart. "And here." He smoothed his palm over her hair. "And that will stop the glow and put things to right."

The girl hugged him tightly then slid to her feet, rushing over to a couple that were standing off to the side and throwing her arms around them as well.

The rest of the kids got up and found their various parents, talking excitedly and tugging their hands. Most likely eager to start their letters.

Everyone applauded as Nick stood, then the crowd began to disperse, and the music kicked up.

"That was quite a story," I told Nick when he came back to me.

"Well…" he shrugged as he trailed off. "Would you like to dance, Ms. Detrich?"

"I'd like that," I agreed.

He led me onto the dance floor, where the remaining couples had congregated, and pulled me into his arms. I lay my head on his chest while we swayed with the music, our fingers entwined, bodies pressed together. It felt so good to just be held by him. I closed my eyes and promised myself that I would allow myself this one moment. Just this, and maybe I could live on the feeling for the rest of my life.

It was so strange to think we'd only known each other, barely, for just a couple days. Standing there in his arms, it felt as if I'd always been there. That odd feeling of home coming in every scent of spruce from his cologne, the feel of his arms closed around my waist, his breath on my neck.

"I should take you home," he said when the song ended, lowering his arms and looking down at me with sadness in his gaze. "Your grandmother will worry."

"I think she knows I'm in good hands," I teased.

"Still." He turned away from me and walked off the dance floor, leaving me to follow in confusion.

I'd thought we were having a moment. Maybe I'd been wrong.

Chapter Eight
~Nick~

I was going to fall in love with her.
I probably already was. The longer I held
her in my arms, the stronger my feelings
for her became. She belonged there, in my
embrace. We fit together like puzzle
pieces, even though we came from
completely different puzzles.

How could fate be so cruel, to put
this perfect human in the path of a
creature who couldn't give her the life she
deserved?

Silence was heavy in the car all the
way back to her house. I didn't know
what to say to her. I worried that if I

opened my mouth only words of
endearment would pour out, and that
wouldn't serve either of us.

I had to go. The longer I stayed
here, the worse it would get. She was
falling for me as well, and if I led her on,
I'd never forgive myself for hurting her
worse than I already was.

When I pulled into her driveway,
she gave me a sad little smile then got out
of the car. I watched her walk toward the
house, knowing with every fiber of my
being that I had to let her go.

But when she turned back to look
at me, my resolve shattered. I opened my
door and got out of the car, striding to her
where she stood staring at me, her eyes
wide with surprise.

My arms wrapped around her waist and I pulled her against me, my lips crashing over hers. She moaned into my mouth, that same sound she'd made in the bakery that first day I met her. The sound having the exact same reaction on my body as it had then. My cock going rock hard against her, our kiss deepening as her arms crossed behind my neck, holding me tightly.

When we pulled apart, I stared at her in wonder as snowflakes clung to her lashes. We both looked around, staring at the snowfall that had seemed to spring up out of nowhere.

"How is it snowing?" she asked, a laugh in her tone. "It has to be almost fifty degrees out here."

I looked back down at her, a pit in my stomach. She was right, it was way too warm for snow.

"Magic," I whispered. I gripped her chin between my fingers and kissed her softly one more time. "I'll call you tomorrow?"

Anya nodded, smiling as she stepped back. She gave me a little wave, then turned and ran up the steps and into the house.

I got back into my car to find my cell ringing in the console where I'd dropped it.

"Hello," I answered, still staring at the house.

"What the hell have you done?" Hela screeched into my ear.

"Excuse me?" I put the phone on speaker as I pulled out of Anya's driveway to head back to the hotel. "What are you talking about?"

"I'm talking about the fact that all hell has broken loose here," she snapped. "The hourglass is glowing bright red, the gates have slammed shut and no one can get in or out, and it's snowing in places it shouldn't be snowing in."

The pit in my stomach grew heavier as the snow started to fall thicker, making visibility lower another mile ahead of the car.

"Why do you think this is something I've done?" I asked.

"The hourglass is red, doofus," she said, a sneer in her tone. "Which means that you've gone and fallen in love."

"What the hell are you talking about?" I slowed the car down, my knuckles white from gripping the steering wheel so hard. It was too warm for the roads to get slick, and the snow certainly wasn't sticking anywhere, but the flakes were so heavy I could barely see anything in front of the car anymore.

"Good lord," Hela said with a sigh. "Santa Claus fell in love. He found his mate. And until you seal the contract, marry her and merge your souls into one...you can't come home."

"That's absurd." I laughed. "Hela, come on. I don't know how you know that I've met someone. But this isn't funny."

"No, it's not funny," she agreed. "How do you not know this?"

"Know what?" I almost missed the entrance for the hotel and had to slam on the brakes to avoid driving past the turn off. I eased the car over and headed toward the parking lot, turning the car off and leaning back in my seat. "I literally have no idea what you're talking about."

"You've started a chain reaction at the Pole," Hela said, exhaling loudly into the receiver. "Your magic is tied to the magic here. This place has always been like…the other half of your soul. Because you've always been alone. But now, you've met someone, your actual soulmate if I'm not mistaken. Until you tie your magic to hers, you can't come back. And none of us can get out."

"What if she doesn't have magic?" I asked, my brow furrowing.

"You fell in love with a mortal?" She cackled so hard I could imagine her actually slapping her knee and rocking back and forth as she did when she found something incredibly funny. "Oh, God, bro, of course you did."

"Shut up," I snapped. "None of this can be true, Hela. How would I not know about it?"

"You've never been interested in love before," she said. "And I'm betting you never read any of your own lore."

"Yeah, I think I skipped the written exam on myself," I agreed, rolling my eyes. "So, what does this mean, exactly?"

"It means you have to marry her. Do you even listen to me when I speak?"

"But what does it mean for her?" I clarified. "She's a mortal."

"She won't be when you marry her." Hela sighed. "Okay, maybe I'm using words that are too big for your tiny little brain. Listen to me. You are soul mates. When you marry, or…you know—"

"Stop. Got it." I shuddered. I was not about to discuss anything remotely close to sex with my little sister.

"Your souls will combine, and she will be immortal. Like you. Because are you listening? Your souls...will mate."

Oh. Well, that was something.

"Okay, so I have to convince a woman that I've just met to marry me and become immortal and move to the North Pole when she doesn't believe in magic and certainly doesn't know that I'm Santa. That's what you're telling me right now?"

"He gets it!" Hela yelled. "Yes. And soon would be great. Christmas is twenty-seven days away. So, your timing is impeccable."

Right.

Fuck.

Chapter Nine
~Anya~

The strange snowstorm that had sprung up was over by time I woke up the next morning. It was still warm out, so thankfully nothing had stuck.

When I went downstairs, Gran was already at the kitchen table, her laptop open as she browsed Black Friday sales. I kissed the top of her head on my way to get a cup of coffee.

"How was your night, dear?" she asked, closing the computer to look at me as I sat across from her.

"It was lovely," I admitted, hiding my smile behind my mug.

It had been better than lovely. Kissing Nick had been more amazing than I'd ever expected kissing could be. We fit so well together, and when I'd felt him hard against me, it was all I could do not to grind myself against him. Somehow I'd gone from no interest in men, to laser focused on this man.

I loved him.

It made no sense. It was so fast, and I still didn't really know him, but it didn't matter. I knew the moment our lips touched, that I wanted to spend the rest of my life with him.

"Will you be seeing more of Mr. Kring?" she teased.

"I certainly hope so," I agreed. "He's a nice man." I tilted my head as I looked at her. "Does it bother you?"

"What dear?" Her brow furrowed.

"He's quite a bit older than me." I shrugged.

"Darling." Gran reached across the table and patted my hand gently. "First of all, it doesn't surprise me in the least that you would gravitate to someone older. You've always been an old soul. Second, in this town…things like age don't really matter to most people. It's all relative."

"Why does everyone talk about this town like it's a living entity?" I asked with a laugh. "The magic of this place…is it really so different here than other places?"

"You have no idea," Gran said, smiling softly at me. "Though I am surprised your new friends haven't explained anything to you."

"Why don't you explain it to me?" I asked her, narrowing my gaze at her. "I feel like I'm missing something huge that's right in front of my face."

"When the time is right," Gran assured me. "It will all become clear. It always does. Now, what are your plans for today?"

"I don't have any," I admitted. Nick said he'd call at some point, but that wasn't really a plan. "How about you?"

"Lunch with the girls, then Bingo tonight." She smiled. "I'm sorry I've been so busy. I know you came here to spend time with me."

"Don't be silly," I insisted. "I'm glad you have a full life here. You don't have to entertain me. I'll be here for a while if that's still okay."

"You can stay forever my darling girl." She beamed at me. "But you can go whenever and wherever you like. All I've ever wanted is for you to be as happy as I've been."

"This place is very special, isn't it?" I asked, really studying her face.

"It really is," she agreed. "And I think Nick is very special, too. If it's right, don't fight it. That's all I ask."

"Why would I fight it?" I asked, surprised.

If anything, I expected Nick to fight whatever was happening between us. He knew he had to leave, and I'd been stunned when he'd finally kissed me. I thought for sure he would leave town with a million things left undone and unsaid between us.

"I don't know," she said, waving her hand dismissively. "Just being a strange, old lady. Don't mind me." She stood up and took her dishes to the sink. "I'm going to head out, get some shopping done before lunch."

"Okay," I said. "Have a nice day."

I was once again struck by how young and vibrant Gran seemed. Even her face seemed less lined and care worn. Like a beautiful Portrait of Dorian Grey, she seemed to be reverse aging before my eyes.

Or maybe I was just noticing it less as I got older. I shrugged and went back upstairs to shower and dress for the day. It looked like I had another afternoon on my own.

****

"Thank you for agreeing to lunch," Nick said as he held out my chair for me. "Sorry for the short notice."

"No, it's fine," I assured him.

When I'd gotten out of the shower I found a text from Nick asking me if I could meet him at the local Mexican restaurant for lunch.

I'd been a little surprised when I'd shown up and was escorted to a private room at the back of the place but couldn't help getting a little excited when I walked in to find Nick already sitting there waiting for me.

We ordered drinks, then food, then the waiter left us alone, closing the door behind himself.

"This is fancy," I said, looking around the small room.

"I just didn't want to be overheard," he said.

He looked almost nervous, and some of my excitement began to turn to fear. God, was he going to break up with me? Could you break up with someone you weren't really dating?

"What's up?" I asked, my posture tightening with tension.

"I need to tell you some things," he said, his hand covering mine on the table. "And I don't know how you're going to react."

"You're married," I whispered, pulling my hand away.

"What?" His brow furrowed. "No. Jesus, Anya. Quite the opposite, actually."

"The opposite would just be not married," I said, relaxing a little.

"The opposite would actually be never having been with any woman ever." He shrugged. "Which is the case. But not what I wanted to talk to you about."

"Wait," I shifted in my chair as I stared at him. "How is that possible?"

"What?"

"You've never been with a woman? Ever. Like…ever?"

"No," he said, shaking his head. "Again, not the point."

"How old are you?" I asked, unable to get past this information. "I mean, that's amazing, and it makes me feel very special. Or it would, if we had ever…which of course, we haven't. You know. Because you were there. Or not."

I was babbling now, and I couldn't seem to get my mouth to stop running. What the hell was wrong with me?"

"Anya!" he snapped, softening his tone with a smile. "Focus, please."

"Sorry," I mumbled. "Please, continue."

"Funny that you should ask how old I am," he continued. "Older than you'd believe, actually. That is closer to what this conversation is going to be about."

"You think I'm too young for you." I nodded.

"I do, yes," he agreed. "But—"

"Don't you think I should be the one to decide—"

"Anya Detrich, if you don't stop talking right this second I'm going to turn you over my knee," he said, exasperated.

"That's not much of a deterrent."

We stared at each other for a moment, the words that had tumbled from my lips hanging between us like a tangible thing, waiting for one of us to pounce on it. My cheeks flamed with heat and I dropped my gaze to the table as his deep chuckle washed over me.

"You're very special to me," he said, turning our hands and entwining our fingers together. "And if the situation were different I would court you properly. I would attempt to win your heart in a more traditional way."

Nick already had my heart. I opened my mouth to tell him so, but the look he gave me made me close my lips. He was right, I needed to stop interrupting. There was obviously something important he was trying to say, and I needed to just let him say it.

A knock came on the door then, the waiter coming back with our food. He placed our plates on the table, refilled our drinks, then slipped out. I wasn't sure if he had felt the tension between Nick and I, but he certainly didn't dawdle.

"As I was saying," Nick continued. "You're very special to me. I didn't actually realize how special until last night. When I kissed you, and it started snowing."

"That was crazy," I admitted. "I've never seen snow pop up in weather this warm."

"Indeed," he agreed. "It was my doing. Not on purpose, of course. But when I kissed you…I put a series of events into motion that I didn't even know were possible."

"What?" I stared at him, completely unsure what he was talking about.

"I told you last night that it was magic, that caused the squall. It was."

"Was what?"

"Magic," he repeated. "My magic."

I sat there, waiting for the punchline, but nothing followed those words. Silence hung in the air, like a pinata waiting to be smashed by one of us. Finally, I couldn't take it anymore.

"What the hell are you talking about?"

"I was born seventeen hundred years ago," he said. "Well, not born so much as…created."

Oh, God. He was crazy. How had I not noticed that he was absolutely insane? Had something happened to him today? A bump on the head? Was he drunk?

"Okay," I said slowly. "I'm going to need a little more than that."

"The story I told the children last night, about the hourglass…that's true. It is there, and it is glowing. It's a warning that if you and I don't…complete what we've started, Christmas will not continue."

"Well," I said, standing up quickly. "That's…I mean…I have to go."

"Don't," he begged, jumping to his feet and reaching for my hand.

I pulled away from him, backing toward the door. I didn't think he was dangerous, but who knew, really? I hadn't realized he was insane until this moment. Who knew what else I'd misjudged?

"Who are you?" I asked him, my hand closing over the doorknob. "Who are you really?"

His shoulders slumped and his bright, blue eyes darkened, a frown pulling at his lips as he met my gaze.

"I'm Santa Claus."

"Santa Claus," I repeated, one last ditch effort to let him hear how absolutely crazy he sounded. "You think you're Santa Claus?"

"Anya, don't go, please. Let me explain."

"You think you're Santa Claus?" I asked one last time.

"Yes."

"Goodbye, Nick." I opened the door and walked as calmly as I could out of the restaurant.

I was almost to my car when a large, black S.U.V. pulled up next to me, the window rolling down to reveal Trudi's smiling face.

"Get in," she insisted, unlocking the doors.

"Now's not a good time," I said, blinking back tears.

"Now is the only time," Candi said, rolling down the window in the back seat. "Get in the car."

I blew out a sigh and walked around to get into the passenger seat. I wasn't in the mood for this, but maybe having friends around me would help with the aching pain in my chest.

"Where are we going?" I asked as I fastened my seatbelt.

"To the bar, of course," Mindi said happily from the seat behind me.

"I'd really rather not," I whined. "I've just had a very upsetting afternoon."

"We know," Trudi said as she put the car in gear and pealed out of the parking lot.

"No, you don't," I argued.

"Actually," Candi said softly. "We do. I'm aware that you don't know us very well, but you're going to have to trust us."

I blew out a snort. The last person I'd trusted had just told me he was Santa Claus and Christmas was about to be canceled.

At least the day couldn't get any weirder from here.

Chapter Ten
~Nick~

"So, maybe not your finest hour," Colton said as he walked into the room with two beers in his hands. "Don't worry, my wife will fix it."

"It was awful," I admitted, accepting the drink as he sat in the chair that Anya had just vacated.

"Well, what did you expect, old boy?" Colton laughed. "Did you just tell her you were Santa Claus and expect her to ask when you wanted to get married? She's a normal. It's going to take some time for her to understand."

"I don't have time," I insisted.

"True." He nodded. "But honestly, I don't know if there was a right or a wrong way to handle the situation. You told her the truth. Now you just have to wait for her to accept it."

"And if she doesn't?" I raised an eyebrow at him.

"Have some faith, Nick. I know it doesn't always feel like it, but fate actually does know what it's doing. There's a reason you met her here, now. She's the one. Just keep that in your heart and the rest will fall into place."

"How can you be so sure?"

"Because six years ago, three sisters showed up in my town, after being on the run from a group of mortals that tried to burn them alive in their home. They all met their eternal mates. And now our magic, along with the magics of a hundred other supernatural creatures has infused this town and brought normals to our side."

"Just like that," I said, saluting him with the neck of my beer bottle before taking a swig.

"No, not just like that. But eventually...yeah. Just like that." He smiled. "Nick, she'll come back."

"How can you be so sure?" I stared at him, waiting for some kind of wisdom. He was over a thousand years younger than me. A werewolf with limited experience outside of the walls of this town. But right now, I was clinging to his every word like he was my own personal Yoda.

"I can't," he admitted. "But I have faith. And you should, too. You're freakin' Santa Clause, dude. If you don't have faith in the power of Christmas, what the hell are the rest of us supposed to do?"

I rolled my bottle between my hands and sighed. For the first time ever, I wished I could get drunk. It seemed like it might be freeing right about now. Just drown my sorrows and forget everything for a little while.

"She's with Trudi?" I asked.

"And Candi and Mindi," he assured me. "They'll explain everything. We probably should have let them do it from the start. Women will believe other women before they ever believe us."

"I love her," I told him, meeting his gaze. "I think I loved her the moment I saw her."

"Your magic recognized her," he said with a shrug. "That's how it is sometimes. You waited a long time for her, Nick. You can wait a little more."

He was right. I knew Anya was the one. And deep down, she knew it, too. I may not have handled telling her the best way I could have, but she deserved to hear the truth from me.

If the triplets were able to convince her that I wasn't crazy I would be eternally grateful to them. And if they could help me get back to the Pole before Christmas, their kids were going to have a hell of a holiday to look forward to.

My phone rang and I didn't have to look to know it was Hela. She'd been calling me every two hours to update me on the state of nothing had changed.

"Do you mind?" I asked, holding up the phone.

"No, do you want me to step out?" Colton asked, already getting to his feet.

I shook my head and waved him back down as I put my sister on speakerphone.

"I'm here with Mayor Steele," I answered. "What's up?"

"Well the fact that you're still there is worrisome," Hela said in an exasperated tone. "You haven't nailed this down yet."

"I haven't nailed anything," I snapped. "Look, I would imagine that you will be the first to know if and when I get this cleared up. You have to stop calling me constantly. I'm working on it, okay?"

"Work faster," Hela said. "Mayor, I look forward to being able to leave this place again so I can come meet you in person. Nick has had nothing but lovely things to say about you and your town."

"Thank you ma'am," Colton said, grinning at me. "I look forward to meeting you."

"Yeah," Hela said. "Hopefully sooner than later. Bro, figure it out. Tick tock."

She hung up and I sighed as I dropped my phone on the table.

"What happens if Anya doesn't marry you before Christmas?" Colton asked. "Can your sister cover for you?"

"Well, there are things that they can do in my absence, of course. All of Christmas wouldn't actually be ruined. But our magics are different. Things that have to be done by Santa, won't be done. The kids in the most need will be the ones who are let down. I can't let that happen." I shook my head and sighed. "What a mess I've gotten myself into."

"It will work out," Colton said again, reaching out to punch me in the shoulder. "There's enough supernatural power in this town to cover a lot of ground. If you need us, there's not a creature within a hundred miles that wouldn't pitch in to help you save Christmas."

"That's...incredibly kind," I admitted, unable to hold back a smile. "You've got a hell of a community here, Colton."

"I'm pretty proud of it," he agreed.

We knocked bottle necks together and finished our beers in silence. I hoped that wherever Anya was now, she wasn't too angry with me. Hopefully Colton was right, and the girls could convince her that I was sincere. If not...well, I might be relying on the kindness of a lot of strangers come Christmas Eve.

Chapter Eleven

~Anya~

"This is unbelievable," I said, staring down at the triplets in amazement. "Witches?"

"Yes, ma'am," Candi assured me as she lowered me back to my feet. "Sorry about that. Quickest way, really."

I'd been trying to walk out of the hotel bar that the girls had closed for a private party after they'd attempted to convince me that Nick really was Santa Claus, when I was suddenly floating above the floor.

"This can't be happening," I said as I dropped into a chair and accepted a beer from Mindi. "Magic is real?"

"Totally real," Trudi agreed. "Five years ago, the magic of Fayshore revealed all of the supernatural creatures to the normals in town. The legend was, when the balance was right, the normals and the specials would live together in harmony." She shrugged. "And now we do."

"So, Gran knows?" I asked. "And she didn't tell me?"

"No one talks about it to outsiders. When we have mortal tourists, for families in town, everyone puts on their glamours and behaves themselves. But when it's just us...well, the freaks come out," Candi said. "I'm sure Nick came here to relax and just be as he is. It's a big draw for out of town monsters."

"He's a monster?" I asked, my brow furrowing.

"Well, he's kind of…" Trudi trailed off, turning her gaze to Mindi.

"He's…um, well," Mindi started, sucking her lower lip between her teeth as she deferred to Candi.

"Oh, for fuck's sake," Candi said, throwing her hands up in frustration. "He's a god."

"A god?" I felt my eyes widen in surprise.

"A Norse god," Candi clarified as if that made it less awe inspiring. "Like a mythological creature. Thor and Odin and Santa and…you know, it's all jumbled up in there."

"So, this is all real?" I asked, looking between them again.

It was insane. But it had been hard to deny once they'd lifted me off my feet without a word. Suddenly I remembered the flying lemon at the bar, and I narrowed my gaze at Candi.

"Did you magic a lemon wedge into Mindi's face the other night?"

"Yeah," she said, grinning. "I didn't think you saw that. You were pretty buzzed."

"That was the night I told Nick that I like him," I admitted.

"Do you love him?" Mindi asked softly, her hand resting on my arm.

"I think so." I shrugged. "I don't know. How can you know this soon? And I mean...I'm just a human. Certainly not good enough for him."

"I don't think you're the one who gets to make that call," Trudi interjected. "And it seems to me that fate has very much had her say in this."

"The spark?" I asked, rolling my eyes.

"I was thinking more shutting the gates on the North Pole and risking Christmas to ensure that the two of you end up together." Trudi narrowed her eyes at me. "But sure, let's go with the spark."

"Okay, look..." I blew out a sigh. "I can buy that you guys are witches. And you're married to a vampire, a werewolf and a demon. But come on...Santa Claus?"

"Normals," Candi scoffed. "You used to believe in Santa, didn't you?"

"Yeah, when I was five," I clarified.

"But you won't believe in Nick?" Mindi asked softly. "You fell in love with him. Probably, if you'd be honest with yourself for a minute, in the first moment you met him. That's how magic really works, Anya. Parlor tricks like ours are nothing compared to the power of true love."

This was insane. Absolutely, batshit crazy. I couldn't really be buying into this…could I?

"You should go talk to him," Trudi insisted. "He's probably upstairs by now. Just talk to him. *Listen* to him. Then let your heart decide."

It couldn't be as easy as she was making it sound. Could it? Let my heart decide? That was terrible advice. My heart wanted chalupas and margaritas three times a day.

"I've never even had a boyfriend," I whispered. "How can I know what love is?"

"Well, you know what it's not," Candi said. "That's a pretty good start."

"Wow," Mindi said, turning to stare at her sister. "That was fairly deep coming from you."

"I have my moments," Candi insisted haughtily. Then she flipped Mindi the bird.

"This day is bananas," I said to myself as I got to my feet. "Okay. I'll talk to him."

"We're a phone call away," Mindi assured me as she stood as well. She took my hands in hers and smiled at me. "Just keep your mind and your heart open. The rest will work itself out."

"Thank you," I said, squeezing her hands gently before releasing them. "All of you."

"Go get your guy," Candi said, lifting her chin toward the door.

Yeah.

That was the plan.

Chapter Twelve

~Nick~

"Anya?" When I'd answered the knock on the door, she was about the last person I expected to see in the hall. "Come in."

I stepped back and opened the door wider, letting her into the hotel room.

She looked around the suite, her arms crossed and her hands rubbing over her biceps nervously.

"Not that I'm not thrilled you're here," I said, motioning for her to sit at the small table in the kitchenette. "But…I'm a little surprised to see you."

"I just left Trudi, Mindi and Candi," she said. "They explained some things to me. Some…very, very strange things. And I thought maybe I should give you another chance to explain."

"What exactly did they tell you?" I asked, unsure where to start.

"That you're a god." She tilted her head and studied my face. "That you really are Santa Claus and that I'll destroy Christmas if we don't have sex tonight."

I sputtered, my eyes going wide in shock. It took me a moment to realize she was kidding. That was good. If she could tease me, then I hadn't completely lost her.

"Okay," she admitted with a soft smile. "Not exactly like that. But it's kind of how it feels."

"I'm sorry," I told her. "I didn't want to have to tell you like this. And I certainly never intended to scare you or to hurt you."

"Do you love me?" she asked, tears glittering in her eyes.

"I do," I said immediately.

"I love you, too," she said. "That scares me, Nick. More than the magic, the Santa stuff, the witches and vampires and werewolves. We don't know each other."

"I know," I whispered. "I swear to you, I didn't even know this could happen. The last thing I want to do is trap you into an eternity of unhappiness. If you aren't ready, if you're never ready, I won't force you."

"You would allow Christmas to disappear?" she asked.

"I would give up everything for you."

Her breath hitched and she shook her head, closing her eyes as a tear rolled down her cheek.

I reached up without thinking, brushing the moisture away with my thumb. Her hand caught mine and she pressed her cheek into my palm as the tears fell harder.

"This is a lot," she said, laughing softly. "Really, Nick? Santa?"

"Yeah," I said, shrugging when she opened her eyes to look at me again. "It's a job."

"It's your life," she argued. "And, if I can be selfish for a moment, what about me? If we do…um, get married, you'll live forever. And I'm just a human girl, with a human lifespan."

"Well, I didn't actually have a chance to get to that part earlier," I said, sucking in a breath. "If you do agree to…marry me…you would also become immortal."

"Of course," she said, her laugh turning cold. "How silly of me."

"What made you come here?" I asked her, unable to hold back the question. "Why did you come to see me tonight?"

"I love you," she said. "I don't like it. I don't know that I want it. But I can't deny it. My thoughts are consumed by you. I've spent my entire life alone. Which is nothing compared to what you've lived, of course. But you were my first kiss. I thought you'd be my first everything." She sighed. "I want you to be my first and last everything. But I'm scared, Nick. The last twenty-four years is a literal lifetime for me...I can't even fathom an actual forever."

"I know," I promised her, sliding off my chair and kneeling at her feet. "Anya, I know. And I can tell you how sorry I am until the end of time, and it won't be enough. But this is who I am.

146

What I am. I'm a man, in love with a woman. An amazing, beautiful, smart, funny woman. I'm just a man, Anya, asking you to spend your life with me."

"Asking me to save Christmas," she corrected.

"No." I shook my head. "I would walk away from all of it. I would find a way to become mortal if that's what you needed me to do. Because none of this is about what I am. About what my job is. This is about us. I would love you in any circumstance, at any point in time, any place in the world. I just want to be with you."

"That is by far," she said, squeezing my hands in hers. "The most saccharine Hallmark card crap I've ever heard in my life."

"I thought it was sweet," I said stiffly as I got back up and returned to my chair. "Not a declaration kind of girl, huh?"

"That's just it," she said, sliding forward and putting her hands on my thighs. "I don't know what kind of girl I am. Because I've never done any of this before, Nick."

"Neither have I," I promised her. "Most preternatural creatures mate for life, Anya. The fact that I've never touched another woman in my life is not unusual among my kind. You were my first kiss, as well. Will be my first everything."

"Will it hurt?" she whispered, dropping her gaze and folding her hands in her lap.

"What?" I stared at her even though she wouldn't look back up at me. "Uh, sex?"

"No!" She shot me a glare. "When you make me immortal. Will it hurt?"

"Oh, I don't know. I don't think so." I shrugged. "I could ask, I guess."

"Ask who?" Her brows furrowed together. "You mean you don't know how to do this?"

"I literally didn't know anything about this until last night," I admitted. "I tried to tell you that earlier. I didn't know this was possible. After I kissed you, my sister, Hela, called me to tell me that the Pole was going crazy and I had to marry you, or I couldn't go home."

"How did you not know this was a thing?" she asked, her tone thick with amusement. "Shouldn't you know about yourself better than anyone?"

"That was Hela's opinion as well." I sighed. "Anya, I don't want you to feel pressured into this. This is literally forever we're talking about here."

"Yeah," she said, smiling softly. "That's the part I do understand. I'm sorry that I didn't believe you."

"I'm shocked you believe me now," I said with a chuckle. "It has to sound crazy."

"It does," she agreed, then tilted her head. "And it doesn't. I've known since I got here that there was something off about this place. My grandmother seems to be getting younger every day. The people are too nice, too close, too…much. The magic of Fayshore, I've been told." She giggled. "God, it was right in front of my face the whole time."

"You don't have to make a decision tonight," I told her. "Or tomorrow. You can have as long as you need."

"I'm good," she said. "Just don't break my heart, okay?"

"I literally couldn't if I wanted to," I promised her. "Once you're mine…you're mine. Our souls will mate, and we'll be together forever."

"And we have to live at the North Pole?" she asked, chewing her lower lip nervously.

"We can live wherever you wish," I assured her. "I'm Santa Claus. If I can fly all over the world in a single night, I don't think a commute to work is going to be too much of a hardship on me. Especially if I know that I'll be coming home to you."

"This is insane," she said, shaking her head.

"The magic?" I asked.

"No. The fact that I want it. All of it. All of you." She smiled, a final tear slipping down her cheek. "That I want forever."

"Are you sure?" I asked. "There's no going back from this."

"Do you want me to change my mind?" she asked, raising an eyebrow at me.

"No," I assured her as I got to my feet. "I absolutely do not."

Chapter Thirteen

~Anya~

I was on my feet and in his arms in the space of a breath. Our lips met and I swear I could feel his magic wash over me. Tingling sparks danced along my skin as the kiss turned deeper, more desperate, our hands roaming each other's bodies as we stood in the kitchen of his hotel room in our passionate embrace.

"Forever?" I asked again, backing away to meet his twinkling gaze.

"Forever," he promised. "I love you."

Then his mouth was on mine again and he scooped me into his arms, carrying me through the room before laying me gently on the bed, his body moving over mine, hips resting between my thighs, our kiss never breaking.

I could feel him hard against my body and I canted up into him, instinctively creating the friction my body was aching for.

Nick moaned into my mouth, his hands sliding up my sides, dragging my shirt up until we had to finally break the kiss so he could discard the t-shirt to the floor.

He trailed wet kisses down my throat and over my chest, pulling my bra down and sucking one of my nipples between his lips, his teeth gently grazing the sensitive nub as I arched into him.

My fingers carded into his thick hair, holding him against my chest as our lower halves ground against each other, my skin on fire as my need for him grew moment by moment.

I had no idea that being intimate with someone would feel like this. So consuming, so feverishly hot and almost painful. I never imagined I could want anything as much as I wanted to feel Nick inside of me at that moment.

His kisses moved further down my body, over my stomach, his tongue swirling my belly button as his fingers undid the button on my jeans. I kicked my shoes off then lifted my hips, allowing him to pull my pants and panties down my legs, taking everything and dropping it to the floor as he stared down almost reverently at my suddenly very naked body.

I fought against the desire to cover myself from him. No one had ever seen me naked before, and I felt incredibly vulnerable in that moment. But all of me was about to belong to all of him. I didn't need to hide. I loved him.

"I want to see you, too," I whispered. "Please?"

Nick smiled at me softly, then stripped quickly until he was naked as well. His body was all hard muscle, chiseled planes of smooth skin, with a thin patch of white hair that led a trail down from his belly button to form a small tuft of curls at the base of his erection.

"You don't look anything like your photos," I teased, reaching out for him, silently asking him to come back to me.

"Well, the camera adds a hundred pounds," he assured me as he climbed back over my body, his lips finding mine again as he settled once more between my thighs.

"I love you," he whispered against my mouth, his tongue darting out to swipe at my lower lip.

"I love you, too," I said.

Nick pressed forward gently, his cock spreading my folds and sliding inside of me. With one firm thrust, he broke my innocence, his mouth covering mine and swallowing my soft cry of pain and surprise.

The sensation of electrical currents over my skin returned, and I opened my eyes to see faint glowing lines of blue and green crawling over our bodies. I sucked in a breath at the sight, my gaze lifting to meet Nick's eyes, which were a vibrant, cobalt blue.

"Forever," he whispered, rocking his hips between my thighs, thrusting deep inside of me.

"Forever," I vowed, my hands sliding up his sides, nails digging into his shoulders as his pace increased and he pushed even deeper, his shaft filling me, drawing me closer and closer to release.

The lights surrounding us grew brighter, and when I fell over the edge of orgasm, his name tearing from my throat as my body convulsed and spasmed from the rush of release, they exploded into a haze of white so bright I had to close my eyes against it.

Nick followed closely behind me, his cry of pleasure deep and rumbling, my own body vibrating from the force of it as his cock jerked inside of me, joining us together for all eternity.

He collapsed to the mattress next to me, gathering me into his arms and kissing me deeply. When we had to break apart to catch our breaths, I lay my head on his chest and listened to the steady thump of his heartbeat under my ear.

His phone rang on the nightstand and he blew out a heavy sigh.

"Would you excuse me for just a moment?" he asked, turning to pick up the phone.

I thought he was going to answer it, but instead he bent down and placed it on the floor, then took my shoe and started smashing the cell phone to bits.

"What are you doing?" I asked, laughing as I pulled a blanket over myself and sat up against the headboard, watching him.

"I'll ask for a new one for Christmas," he promised, sitting up next to me.

"Hmm, well, have you been naughty, or have you been nice?" I asked,

162

looking over at him with a soft smile spreading over my lips.

"I'm not sure," he said. "I'll have to ask my wife and get back to you. I'm pretty sure she'd say nice."

I stared at him, my eyes widening as I realized that, magically speaking, we were probably married now. If those lights were what I thought they were, then the process had already started. Hell, might already be done and wrapped up with a nice tidy bow.

"So, am I Mrs. Kring or Mrs. Claus?" I asked him, my smile growing bigger as the words came out.

"Whatever you wish," he said with a shrug. "I go by Kring when I travel, but technically it's actually —"

"Kringle!" I said, laughing. "Oh my God. You're married to an idiot."

"No," he assured me, pulling me into his arms again and kissing me softly. "I'm married to an amazing woman whom I can't wait to spend the rest of eternity with."

"I guess we can start there," I agreed through a yawn.

Nick slid down and pulled me with him, returning us to our previous position of my head on his chest, his arm around me, his lips pressed to my temple.

Yeah, forever was a pretty good start.

Chapter Fourteen

~Nick~

"What time is it?" Anya asked, her tone still thick with sleep.

"I'm not sure," I admitted, blinking to adjust to the dark room. "Late, I think. We must have fallen asleep."

"I should call Gran," she said. "She'll be worried."

"You're an adult," I assured her. "I'm sure she'll be okay until morning. We'll go together first thing. I'd like to ask her for your hand officially anyway."

"Just my hand?" she asked.

I reached over and pinched her side, making her giggle and try to squirm away from me. But when I pulled her close and held her, she settled back down against my chest.

"Happy?" I asked her, kissing her forehead softly.

"Incredibly," she admitted with a sigh. "I do have questions though."

"I'm sure," I said. "Fire away. I've got nowhere else to be."

I felt her lips curl into a smile against me and hugged her tighter for a moment. Gods above, I hoped that I could make her smile like that forever.

"How exactly do you travel to every child's house in the world in one night?"

Somehow I knew she was going to start with a Santa question. Most people did.

"I don't actually have to do that anymore," I told her. "Now, it's more about ensuring that parents are able to get the gifts for their kids. As the world changes, my magic changes, and the tools change. Before electricity and cars and computers, back when people still believed in magic, yes, I hooked up a sleigh and flew around the world, delivering wooden trains and hand sewn dolls to children."

"But not anymore?"

"No," I said with a sigh. "It's a different kind of magic now. Sometimes it's putting the right gift in a parent's path. That impossible to find gaming system suddenly pops up as available when a parent is scrolling late at night on their phone. A hundred-dollar tip is given to a single mom working a second job to give her kid a nice Christmas. An unexpected holiday bonus from a boss that has suddenly been gifted the spirit of the season."

"That's almost more magical," Anya said, her tone full of wonder. "Do you really have a list?"

"I do," I said, smiling at her curiosity. "But truth be told, there's never been a naughty name on it. All children deserve Christmas."

168

"Did you ever visit my house?"

"No," I admitted. "But when you were seven, all you wanted was a first edition of Little Women. And one of my guys dropped it into an estate sale your parents got a nudge to visit on their way to visit a friend."

I felt her tense up in my arms and shifted to look down at her. It was dark, but I could see her outline in shadow against me.

"My parents," she whispered. "Is this one of those Twilight things, where I have to go away and will never see them again?"

"No," I assured her. "There are many options for how we can deal with that. We can use glamours to appear older to them. You could tell them the truth. Or we could ask Booker to turn them and your Gran into vampires."

She laughed, but I could hear tears in it.

"You will not lose your family because of this decision," I promised her. "I won't allow it. I'm not taking you away from your life, Anya. I'm just becoming a part of it. As you are part of mine."

"You're kind of perfect, Nick Kringle."

"I believe it is you that is perfect, Mrs. Kringle." I lay my head on hers and held her close as sleep pulled at me again.

"I think I'd quite like to be Mrs. Claus," she whispered, her fingers trailing up and down my chest.

"Your wish is my command," I said. "Mrs. Claus."

Chapter Fifteen

~Anya~

I woke up to the sound of Nick talking on the phone somewhere in the hotel room. I pulled his shirt on and buttoned it as I walked into the front room, to see him pacing on the hotel phone.

"Yes, Hela," he hissed. "I will be home soon. However, I need a short while longer here with Anya. And I'd appreciate it if you could at least pretend not to know what transpired between the two of us last night. This is a private matter between her and I."

His gaze lifted and met mine, and I could see the apology forming on his handsome face.

Of course, his sister was aware we'd slept together. If it worked as it was supposed to, then things had been set to right at the North Pole the moment we'd...consummated our relationship.

My cheeks heated with embarrassment, but I shook my head at him, silently assuring him that everything was fine. What was done was done. I'd have to get used to this magic stuff eventually.

"I have to go," he said. "Yes, I will replace my phone this afternoon. Though I do suggest that you don't call me again. I will let you know when I'm headed back."

He hung up and walked over to me, pulling me into his arms and kissing me deeply.

"So, she knows, then?" I asked when we broke apart.

"Unfortunately, I believe quite a few people will know." He sighed. "Magic like that doesn't generally go unnoticed in a town like this."

"Of course." I smiled up at him. "It's fine. I'm not ashamed of what we've done. It was the purest declaration of love I could have made to you. I refuse to be overly embarrassed by it."

Until I had to tell Gran anyway. I felt my face fall as I realized that I had no idea how to explain this decision to her. Then again, she lived in a magic community, so maybe it wouldn't be as difficult as I feared.

"Let's get some breakfast," Nick suggested. "Then I'll take you home and we can speak with Evie together."

I nodded. I had a feeling that everything was going to be just a little easier with Nick at my side.

****

"Oh, my darling girl!" Gran said, throwing her arms around me and hugging me tightly. "This is wonderful."

"Really?" I asked, wiping a tear away before hugging her back. "You're not disappointed?"

"Disappointed?" Gran stepped back and beamed at me, then over at

Nick. "Honey, I couldn't be more happy for you. To have found a man that you love, that will love you in return, forever? Well, there's no greater magic in the world."

"Ma'am," Nick said as Gran released me. "I apologize for not asking you first, but I would like to ask you now. May I officially have your granddaughter's hand in marriage?"

"It would be my honor," Gran said, bowing slightly to Nick. "Will there be a wedding?"

Oh. I hadn't even thought of that. I looked over at my husband and he nodded encouragingly.

"Maybe in the spring," I suggested. "Nick obviously has to go back soon."

"Will you be going with him?" she asked.

"I don't think so," I admitted. "He's lost some valuable time and I'm afraid I'd be a distraction."

"A welcome one," Nick assured me, his arm winding around my waist. "But perhaps you're right. I will come back often to visit between now and Christmas, then I'll return for good when things slow down."

"When are you leaving?" Gran asked him.

"The earliest possible tomorrow morning," Nick said, his tone tinged with disappointment.

"I'd like to stay here," I told Gran. "If that's still okay?"

"I've told you that you're welcome here forever," she reminded me with a tsk of her tongue. "And I meant it."

"Thank you." I beamed at her. "We'll be having dinner at the mayor's house tonight. And they've asked that I extend the invitation to you as well."

"How lovely," Gran said. "I'd be honored."

"I'll be back to pick you up at five," I told her. I pulled away from Nick and gave her a kiss on the cheek. "I love you."

"Where are you off to now?" she asked.

"We're going to grab lunch, then Nick has to pack and get ready to leave," I said, fighting to keep sadness out of my tone.

"I'll be back," he whispered, pressing a kiss to my temple.

"I know," I said, shaking my head. "I'm just being silly."

"Well, you two have a nice time and I'll see you both tonight," Gran said as she walked us to the door.

That night I would have dinner with my new Fayshore family. I would say goodbye to my husband and go home with Gran. And I would count down the days to Christmas on my big ships of the Navy calendar. Then, twenty-six days later, Nick would return to me and we would purchase our own home in the Fayshore community. Where our love would add to the magic of this amazing town forever.

It was a comfort to know that I
would always be home for the holidays.

Epilogue

~Nick~

One year later...

"It's not too heavy," I told Anya as we walked through the snow toward the red and white striped pole. "But sometimes it sticks, so just let me know if you want me to help."

"No way," she insisted, smiling at me. "It's my first Christmas here, I want to pull the lever and I'll do it myself."

Normally the whole village will come to watch the turning of the hourglass, but somehow my wife had convinced them to let us have this moment in private. I couldn't imagine why, but I also couldn't deny her anything she wished.

We stood in front of the Pole and I watched the excitement spread across my wife's beautiful face as she reached out her hands to grip it in her palms.

"So, how was your first Christmas here?" I asked her. "Did they make you hot cocoa and force you to watch movies all night?"

"Will you hush?" she hissed. "This is a special moment. I want to enjoy it."

After so many years flipping the hourglass, I really didn't get much pleasure out of it anymore. It was more of a chore than an event. But she was right, if it was important to her I should let her savor it.

"Are you ready?" she asked, leaning back and grinning as the lever began to shift.

"Sure," I said. She was really making this a bigger deal than it needed to be.

Across the town, the hourglass began to flip and with one more hard pull on Anya's part, the lever clicked, and the glass tilted.

Suddenly, the hourglass exploded into bright blue light, the diamonds turning to radiant, glowing sapphires in the top half of the glass.

"What the hell?" I asked, my heart in my throat. This had never happened before, and after last year's panic, I'd kind of hoped to never see that damn thing glow ever again. Even if that had turned out better than I ever could have dreamed.

"Well," Anya said brightly, wiping her hands on her jeans. "That was one hell of a gender reveal, wouldn't you say, honey?"

"Gender reveal?" I turned to stare at her, my brow furrowed in confusion. "What are you…" My gaze lowered down her body to where her hand was resting over her belly. "You're pregnant?"

She nodded and beamed at me, then jerked her chin toward the hourglass.

"I wanted to find a special way to tell you," she admitted. "And I didn't want you worrying through Christmas. So, Hela and I came up with this."

"It's perfect," I told her, pulling her into my arms and swinging her around. "You can't be far enough along to be able to know the sex yet."

"No, I'm only about twelve weeks," she admitted. "But the magic doesn't need an ultrasound, dear. You and I just found out together." She motioned toward the hourglass.

"How did you know it would work?" I asked her, holding her against my chest as I blinked back tears of joy.

"I had faith," she answered. "A boy!"

"A baby!" I agreed.

She lifted her face and I bent down to kiss her. I couldn't believe she'd managed to keep that secret from me. Though, it was my busiest time of year, so maybe I'd been distracted enough for her to get away with it.

"I love you, Mrs. Claus" I told her, cupping her jaw in my palm and staring down into her eyes.

"I love you, too," she promised. "Next week when we head back to Fayshore, I'll have the whole family over so we can tell them together."

"Can you wait that long?" I teased.

"I waited this long to tell you," she said, rolling her eyes. "I can wait another week to send Gran and my mother into shrieks of happiness."

"Speaking of shrieks of happiness," I said, narrowing my gaze at Anya.

"Come on, Santa," she said, her own eyes visibly darkening as she licked her lower lip. "Let's get you to bed."

"Yes, ma'am." I picked her up and threw her over my shoulder as she laughed and kicked her feet.

It was definitely a very, merry Christmas in the Claus house that night.

About the Author

Dakota Rebel is a bestselling author and a very slow distance runner who dreams of racing Badwater.

She lives in a perpetual state of exhaustion with her happy husband and two incredibly spoiled children.

Dakota loves to talk to her readers and can be found at www.dakotarebel.net

Made in the USA
Middletown, DE
22 September 2023

39095687R00118